My Child,
My Love

My Child, My Love

Story — Sue Krupa

Written — Nyle Smith

Illustrated — Douglas Clawson

Cover Design — DeAnne W. Crandall

Edited — Suzanne Brady

To
Rich and Tami
Who through their faith and love
bring miracles to all who know them

and

DeAnne,

Roxanne,

Laura Lee,

Stacy,

Alice,

Ardis and C.J.

Published by
Rag Doll Publishing
Sue Krupa/Kent Smith

Chapter One

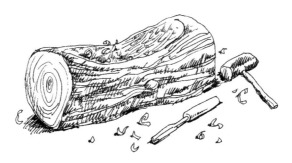

Leah screamed. Pearls of sweat beaded up on her face as she tried to bear the pain.

"Push!"

Leah pushed again, the baby being her central thought and holding her baby the one purpose that had kept her going the past twelve grueling hours. She nearly passed out as she collapsed on the bed. She was exhausted. Her eyes focused on the roughly shaped block of wood next to the bed. Her husband, Daniel, had proudly begun forming the cradle a few weeks ago. He still had a long way to go before it was finished, but he wanted the babe to spend its first moments in a bed carved by his own hands. They hadn't expected the baby for at least another month.

"Push!"

Leah fought for the energy and then pushed again before falling back onto the bed for what seemed the thousandth time. As she struggled for breath, she could hear the faint sounds of the early-morning merchants beginning to hawk their wares in the streets of Bethlehem. Daniel took her hand and turned her face to him.

"We can see the head and shoulders. One more time, and then you'll be able to hold our baby."

"I'm too tired, Daniel, I'm just too tired," mumbled Leah.

Daniel's arms surrounded her, supporting her.

"One more time," he repeated and nodded to his mother.

"Push!" Sarah said again.

Leah pushed, finding a reservoir of strength that could only have been formed from primal elements deep inside her. The baby surged out in a rush of life. Leah cried, and Daniel held her tight in his joy. Sarah raised the little boy, smiling, and lowered the child as she cleared his mouth. She worked on the baby and then looked to Daniel with worry. He rushed to her side, picked up the child and spanked him, trying to get that important first gasp of breath. Nothing. Daniel tried again. Nothing. Leah, only faintly aware of what was happening, looked up to see Sarah wrapping the child in a blanket and moving to the far side of the room. Daniel returned to her side.

"I'm sorry, Leah. I'm so sorry."

Leah turned her face toward the wall, wanting to shut out the hushed sounds behind her, the whispering voices and the hurried movements of her husband and her mother-in-law. She screwed her eyes shut tight, trying not to see the images that assailed her from every corner of her grieving soul. She ignored the hands that caressed her and washed her. She tried not to feel anything as the bedclothes were removed from around her and replaced with fresh ones. She welcomed the new scent and used it as a catalyst to draw her thoughts away from this room, away from the agony, away from the grief. But the memories were even fresher than the scent of the bedclothes, and they came screaming uninvited back into her mind.

She had pushed away the thought of holding her baby, but the desire to feel her child in her arms overwhelmed her. "I want to see my baby," she said softly to Daniel, who was now on his hands and knees scrubbing the floor clean, trying to erase the tragedy that was befalling them. He looked up toward Leah, and then back at his mother. Sarah shook her head. No. Daniel looked at the floor for a few moments and then returned Leah's gaze.

"Leah . . , dear . . , I think it's best if you don't," said Daniel.

"Daniel, I need to see our baby. I need to hold my child," pleaded Leah.

"Daniel's right, dear," interrupted Sarah. "I can't imagine it would do you any good."

Sarah strode out of the room with the child in her arms. Leah watched helplessly. "Daniel," she pleaded again. He scarcely glanced up as he made long strong strokes with the rag in his hand, raising the grain of the plank floor as he forced more and more water into it in his attempt to scrub it clean.

"Daniel, please," Leah said, her voice laden with anguish. "Please . . ."

Daniel scrubbed with renewed vigor, not daring to lift his eyes. Leah dropped back onto the bed, not believing her own loving husband couldn't recognize her absolute need to hold their child before it left their life for good. In a voice laced with agony and heartache, Leah cried, "Bring me my baby! Let me hold my child!"

Daniel, his eyes filling with tears, said, "Leah, it would tear the very life out of me to hold him. If it would do that to me, think what it would do to you."

Leah replied with sudden calmness, "Daniel, if I don't hold that child, I'll no longer have any life left in me, and I've got very little as it is. I thought I'd spend the rest of my life holding him. Please let me have this one moment."

Daniel considered. There was no right in this situation; there seemed nothing but wrong. What would it hurt to let Leah hold their child? Maybe it actually would comfort her. He knew for sure that Leah would never forgive him if he didn't bring her the child now. Daniel struggled to his feet and left the room. Leah lay still, frightened, but certain she was doing what was necessary. She could hear Daniel descend the stairs, heard a hushed and heated exchange of words, and then the stair planks creaked one at a time as he ascended them. The sound of his slow, deliberate steps brought Leah closer to the moment she feared and desired, the moment she had to face. As her husband slumped into the doorway, he looked as weak as a little boy as he stood crying, his tears splashing onto the cloth that wrapped their firstborn.

Daniel walked across the room and sat on the bed next to Leah, silently handing her the bundle of blankets saying nothing. Leah held the bundle as if it were the most precious thing on earth, gently brushing away the blanket that covered the infant's face. The face was that of a little boy with long lashes, ringed by small, tight curls of hair held firmly in place by the remains of the birthing fluids. His nose looked like a doll's, and his tiny mouth was pursed, delicately lined by two perfect lips. Leah raised the child's hand and, in a ritual as old as the earth, counted her baby's fingers. Then she reached down into the blanket and brought out first one small foot and then the other, counting once again to ten as she rolled each tiny toe between her fingers. She didn't allow herself to think that she could keep this child, that somehow the events of the past hours could be erased and rewritten. She held the child's cheek to her own and was startled by the coolness of her baby's skin. The skin that minutes ago was turning from purple to pink was now slowly fading to blue. Leah held him tight, trying to force warmth into him through her own body and the baptism of her warm tears.

Daniel tightened his grip around Leah as he witnessed the sad bonding of mother and son. Desperate for something to say, finally he thought of the words that Leah's own mother had used in times of tribulation, words he himself had used before to comfort Leah when she seemed beyond comforting.

"Faith and love, Leah. With faith and love there is no problem that can't be solved or hurt undone."

Leah held the child tighter to her breast, clutching him as if she were a little girl clutching her doll to ward off the dark. She fought back the urge to reproach Daniel, to ask how he dared use those words to her now, when she was holding her lifeless baby, to ask how stupid and uncaring he could be to reduce this moment to a trite remark. Didn't he understand, couldn't he see with his own eyes, how her very desire to live had been shaken by this tragic event? But she was too fatigued to be angry with him, and she knew he was only searching for a way to comfort her. She drew in a deep breath and let it slide out of her as she felt his caring arms embrace her.

"Daniel," Leah said frailly, "please don't ever say those words to me again. Right now I have no faith, and I find it very hard to find love in a world where things like this can happen."

No matter how softly she uttered them, her words seared Daniel's heart. "Leah, I meant nothing but to offer comfort. If I could change this, I would give my life to do it. I love you, Leah, and we have to live through this. We have no other choice. Please, don't shut me out; let us live through this together."

Leah knew that Daniel was right. This experience was one they could not escape. Yet her anguish was unbearable. She had been taught all of her life about God and his mercy. Where was his mercy now? Where was the miracle she ached for? She wanted to believe that somehow, somewhere, her baby was being taken care of, that even now someone was holding and cherishing him. She wanted to believe it was just a matter of time until she could hold her son again.

Instead, Leah brushed aside a small ringlet of hair from her son's forehead and gently kissed him for the first and last time. She laid her head against Daniel's arm.

"I want him to have a name," she said.

"His name is Benjamin."

Daniel nodded assent.

Leah wrapped her son again in the blanket and held out the precious bundle to unseen hands.

"Please," she prayed, "this is Benjamin. Keep him warm."

Chapter Two

Ardis's sandals skiffed up puffs of dust as she half-skipped and half- ran down the road to Bethlehem. She sang a song that generations of little girls had sung before her as she turned her face to the rising sun, letting its warming rays soak into her olive skin.

The night before, aunts, uncles, and cousins had gathered at her father's shepherd's camp. She didn't really know why they were here, just that it had something to do with the Roman king. Her gathered family grumbled late into the night over something called taxes. She smiled as she remembered her father rising early to slaughter one of the finest sheep, setting aside the choicest cuts for a family feast. "Ha," he said to no one in particular. "This is one less sheep the fat king will taste." She laughed out loud at the spectacle of her father, his own considerable belly spilling out from under his robe, calling someone else fat and doing it with such gusto.

Ardis shifted the bundle strapped to her back, a bundle of some size, filled with carefully wrapped mutton. Six days of the week Ardis made this trip to the inn in Bethlehem. She enjoyed her trips but welcomed the Sabbath so she could rest and be with her family.

Ardis looked forward to seeing Daniel. For nearly a year she had loved him as one of the best grown-up friends a seven-year-old girl could have. He always had a cool drink and something sweet for her to eat, but her favorite part was the jokes that were always quick to trip off his tongue. Ardis was especially comfortable around Daniel because he reminded her of her father, belly and all.

Last month Daniel had asked if she could stay to help straighten up, prepare food, wash bedding, and otherwise help ready the inn for the day's guests. Ardis jumped at the chance. The inn had become a second home to her, and she was needed to help out while Leah recuperated after losing her baby boy.

For a while she didn't see Leah at all. Slowly Leah started coming down from her upstairs bedroom to help when she could. Leah's eyes seemed different to Ardis, as if a fire had dimmed. She kept her distance from Ardis now, whereas before she had been as quick as Daniel to join in a game or to break into song.

One morning Ardis had decided to do something to help bring some light back into

Leah's eyes. She approached Leah just as she was just coming down the stairs.

"Leah," she said, "I know your little boy went to heaven, and you're sad because you can't hold him, but I'm here and you can hug me anytime. Maybe even pretend I'm him."

Daniel looked up quickly from the meat he was chopping. Sarah, who was stoking the fire in the hearth, audibly drew in her breath as she wheeled toward the stairway, afraid of Leah's reaction. Leah, stunned, was softened by the innocent gaze of this small girl who truly believed that this make-believe game could somehow ease her anguish. She wrapped Ardis in her arms and held her, stroking her hair. After a few moments, though, she burst into tears, ran up the stairs to her room and shut the door behind her. Her muted sobs could be heard above the crackle of the fire and the sputtering soup.

Ardis turned helplessly toward Daniel, near tears herself. Daniel knelt and took her hand, ignoring his mother's sharp stare.

"Honey," he said, "don't worry. I know you were just trying to make her feel better, weren't you?"

Ardis nodded yes, the corners of her eyes now translucent with tiny pools of water welling up.

"Thank you, Ardis. It's just that Leah is . ., well . ., very sad right now. Even she doesn't know why she can't stop crying."

Ardis nodded as if she understood, but what she really wanted to do was run out of the inn's front door into the busy streets of Bethlehem.

Daniel could tell she still felt sheepish. Ardis wanted to be anywhere but the inn at that moment. "Why don't we call today a free day?" Daniel offered. "You can just go and see whatever you want here in town and then go home when you feel like it. I'll even pay you for today. You can't find a better deal than that." He hugged her as she hesitated for a moment and then released her. Ardis burst out the door, seeking refuge in the sun.

Daniel avoided the reproachful stare of his mother. He knew she thought the child had

MY CHILD, MY LOVE

overstepped her bounds and that his words should have been sharper. He finally turned toward her and said, "Mother, she's just a little girl who wanted to help. This world could use a few more just like her." Sarah huffed and left the room.

When Ardis returned the next day, Leah greeted her with a full breakfast. Ardis grinned, ate, and put the whole experience behind her with the ease only a seven-year-old can muster.

Now, on this particular morning, Ardis grew more excited with every skip and every step that carried her closer to the inn. She had a gift for Leah hidden in her tunic, a gift she was sure would cheer her.

Ardis sprinted the final fifty yards to the inn, bursting through the door out of breath and with a big grin on her face. Daniel was at the table, finishing his breakfast. Ardis momentarily forgot her package as she remembered her father that morning. She blurted out, "Are you fat?" Daniel choked on his last bite of food, half in shock and half laughing. Sarah, preparing bread at the table, huffed loudly and glared at Daniel, hoping he would put this impertinent girl in her place.

"Why would you ask that?" sputtered Daniel, his eyes dancing in amusement.

"I was just wondering if the king is fatter than you and my father. It seems he must be, " Ardis continued. "Otherwise, why would everyone bring so much food to feed the king?"

"Ah," Daniel chuckled, "now I understand. Probably he is, although I've never seen the king. I do know he doesn't eat everything. In fact, he sells most of it to make money."

"You mean he doesn't have to work?" asked Ardis.

"Not like you and I have to."

"That's not fair. We work for our food. Why do we have to give it to him?" Ardis asked indignantly.

"That's a question all of us ask, Ardis."

"Actually," said Sarah, "it's best for little girls not to talk so much or ask too many questions."

"At least that's one opinion," Daniel retorted, "but you can always ask me anything you want, Ardis, and if I know the answer, I'll tell you. Now let's get to work."

"Is Leah coming down this morning?" asked Ardis excitedly as she fingered the bundle at her waist.

"Maybe in a little while," replied Daniel.

Ardis started to sweep the floor, well away from where Sarah was kneading her dough. Sarah watched to make sure Ardis didn't kick up any dust near the food. Her cooking was known all over Bethlehem. Guests most often came through her doors after asking a town person where to find a good meal and a clean bed for the night. Structurally the inn was nothing special to look at, but it was solid and built to last for centuries. Sarah loved her son more than life, and Daniel knew that because he was the only one, besides his late father, whom she had allowed past her outer veneer.

Daniel carefully watched Ardis to make

sure she didn't get near his mother. Ardis seemed especially giddy this morning, as she danced with the broom, whirling about the room. Leah, watching unnoticed from the top of the stairs, looked at Ardis with both joy and pain. She couldn't help but think that her own baby, her little Benjamin, would have been this full of life, finding joy in even the mundaneness of daily living. Her own joy had seemed to end when she greeted and said farewell to her lifeless baby boy with the same anguished kiss. Leah longed for the day when she could feel happy again, when the sight of a beautiful morning would fill her with joy, the small satisfactions of life coming at the turn of every hour of the clock. She feared it would never be so again.

Leah's gaze turned to her mother-in-law. Sarah was a good woman, a woman who had raised her son correctly. She, too had suffered much in her life. Daniel had come as a miracle in Sarah's life after her first two children were stillborn. Leah couldn't help but think that Sarah's experiences would surely now give them common ground though the two women had never talked much to each other. Leah knew that Daniel didn't know what to do in the situation either. He loved both of them and hoped that something one day would bring his wife and mother closer together.

Leah started down the stairs. Ardis looked up with anticipation. She threw down the broom and rushed halfway up the stairs to give Leah a hug.

"Well, this is a welcome greeting," said Leah, trying to push past her own troubles to share the joy of the day with Ardis.

"I have something special for you," said Ardis as she tore at the bundle under her tunic, nearly ripping it in the process.

"Here, let me help you," said Leah as she knelt, carefully untangling the bundle from Ardis's waistband. Ardis took something out of the bundle and hid it from Leah's view.

Ardis, the smiles bubbling out of her, said, "It's not supposed to be your baby. It's just something to hold and love." From behind her back, Ardis produced a small rag doll that looked as if it had seen many a day being dragged through the dirt and many a night being held tight by a little girl who truly loved her dolly. Little of the original doll remained, for new rags had been added wherever the old ones had become too tattered, and new arms and legs were rewrapped in new scraps as they were unraveled by time. For just a moment, Leah entertained the ironic thought that she too was a rag doll, torn and tattered and rewrapped a few too many times when life had unraveled her.

"I'll miss her, because I've loved her a long time. I want you to have her now because you need her more than I do," said Ardis hopefully, but as soon as she said it, she regretted it. When it came to actually giving up her doll, Ardis suddenly knew she would spend restless nights with empty arms. She had never slept without her doll. "It's been my baby ever since I was a baby," she continued. "My momma made her for me. She's a big comfort during the night."

The room was absolutely silent while

Daniel and Sarah watched. Daniel waited for the certain outcry from Leah. Instead, he watched in gratitude as Leah took the doll from Ardis and clutched it tightly to her breast. Her tears were large and gentle. It was a few moments before she reluctantly pulled the doll away from her and placed it back in Ardis' arms.

"I can't take your baby, dear. Babies need to be with their mothers, and mothers need to be with their babies."

Ardis was relieved but still a little disappointed. "I know, but I just wanted you to be with my baby because you can't be with yours."

Leah hugged both Ardis and her rag doll. "Thank you, Ardis. Thank you for sharing your baby with me." As Leah hugged her, a few tears spilled down Ardis's back, and then none. Even Sarah was touched by the display, and both she and Daniel were silently relieved as the moment passed peacefully.

"It's a beginning," thought Daniel to himself.

Chapter Three

Bethlehem held a special place in the hearts of the Jewish faithful, because it was prophesied that the Messiah himself would rise from Bethlehem to lead his people. Even though the census filled the city to capacity, there was still a serene beauty that could be felt by those who took the time to feel it. Roman law was very specific that returning to one's ancestral home for the census was not necessary. The Romans were happy to tax people wherever they lived. It was Jewish law that required the faithful to return home for census. Bethlehem was a city that many a family prided themselves in claiming as their ancestral home.

Against Bethlehem's tapestry of ancient serenity and current bustle stood the inn, a plain building that portrayed a sense of character and a simple, peaceful beauty. Only those walking close by could see the simple wooden wall that shielded a cavelike stable. Several small bushes fought to keep their place in the arid ground about the inn, but the eye was drawn to a few green branches jutting out from behind the inn, the branches of an ancient olive tree that had not been pruned for a century.

Beneath this tree Daniel knelt near a small stone marker next to a larger marker. His fingers caressed the earth as he brushed away leaves and other debris from around the marker. With great effort he stood and then knelt again, this time beside the larger marker. He repeated the cleaning of the ground, as if it were a sacred ritual. He clapped his hands to rid himself of the dust, and for just a few moments the dust hung in the air about his head as if it were a halo in the sunlight. Daniel lumbered to his feet again, walked to the base of the tree, and slid his back down the trunk until he was seated on the ground. He stretched out his legs and crossed them and then crossed his arms across his chest as he settled back against the tree. He was silent for a moment and then turned to the larger marker as if he were speaking to an old friend.

"We're counting on you to take good care of him," Daniel said.

He waited a few moments, as he always did, on the chance his mother-in-law would speak back to him from the grave. She didn't, and Daniel sighed and looked at the window of a small room near the back corner of the inn and remembered...

"You see how the branches reach up like

arms?" asked Elisabeth, Leah's mother. "You know who they're reaching to, don't you?"

Leah scrutinized the tree limbs, as if the answer lay somewhere in the rough bark and the odd gnarled knot, but no answer presented itself to her ten-year-old mind.

"How about you, Daniel? Do you know?" asked Elisabeth.

Daniel leaned out the window as far as he could to see the branches better. He wanted to come up with the right answer, not only to please Elisabeth but also to show Leah how mature he was at eleven, a whole year older than she was. As he looked more closely at the tree, he lost his grip on the window ledge and fell face first toward the ground some fifteen feet below him. He would never forget the feeling of Elisabeth's hand, grabbing his foot at the last moment and saving him from certain destruction. His father, Jacob, heard the noise and rushed out of the stable, reaching up to gently lower his son to the ground.

Daniel fought back tears as he buried his

face in his father's chest. Leah mustn't see him cry. He was embarrassed enough as it was by falling out of the window. He closed his eyes, forcing the tears back, and waited a moment to catch his breath as the fear passed from him. When he thought he could put on a brave face again, Daniel unburied his face and looked up, the branches of the tree framing the faces of Elisabeth and Leah as they peered down from above.

"Who?" Daniel yelled.

"What?" replied Elisabeth, her heart still racing from the whole episode.

"Who are the branches reaching up to?" Daniel asked.

"God," she said. "They're reaching up to God."

Elisabeth laughed in relief.

"Maybe to catch his angels," chimed in Leah, "like your father just did."

As Daniel felt the arms of his father squeeze him tight, he looked up again and saw the face of Leah and hoped he could catch her if she ever fell. Daniel was sure she was one of God's angels.

"The branches that don't reach up are reaching out like God's love, providing shelter and a place for us to rest when the world becomes too hot and unbearable," continued Elisabeth. "After a while, we're rested and ready to face the world again. Come to think of it, those branches reaching out are a lot like your inn, Jacob."

Elisabeth didn't know it at the time, thought Daniel as he was brought back to the present by the beginnings of a cramp in his back, but those words drove him to keep the inn going, even when it seemed impossible to do so. Someone had to reach out like those old branches and provide shelter, and it might as well be he. It was serendipity that brought Leah to work beside him not only in the inn but in life as well.

He shifted positions as he remembered how happy he had been as a boy to see Elisabeth and Leah two or three times a year. The inn was a peaceful place of refuge for them after Elisabeth's husband died when Leah was only seven. The back guest room, which overlooked the tree, was always theirs when they came.

Years later, it was to this small room that Elisabeth and Leah had come for refuge when Elisabeth had become ill. Daniel was a young man now, and his father had passed on years before, leaving Daniel and his mother the task of keeping the inn.

"I want to be buried under that tree," Elisabeth said to Leah and Daniel as they lifted her to the window one afternoon so she could see the tree and smell the afternoon breeze. Elisabeth looked up to Daniel. "I know it's against tradition. Perhaps it's asking too much."

Daniel looked from her eyes into the tear-filled eyes of Leah and knew this was a request he couldn't deny.

"Of course you can be buried there," he said. "After all, that's what the tree is there for, isn't it? To hold angels like you."

Soon after, Elisabeth lapsed into the coma from which she never awakened. In the months it took for Leah's mother finally to be released from this life, Daniel had gave them both free room and board. After her mother's death, Daniel asked Leah to stay and help run the inn in exchange for room and board. Leah knew he didn't need her help, that it was his kindness which made the offer. But she had no place else to go, and the inn had a warm and comforting atmosphere. She could feel her mother's love in the guest room overlooking the tree, like the scent of a flower lingering after it withers.

Leah soon grew to love Daniel for his goodness and caring. He was a man she could trust, a man who would stay beside her, a man who would make an excellent father. It was comical what she had to do to catch his eye. Unbeknownst to her, however, she had had his heart from the moment she first walked into the inn as a child years before. Yet Daniel doubted that she would ever love him that is, until the day she calmly cornered him and asked him how long it was going to take for him to ask her for her hand.

Sarah was by no means pleased with the arrangement. First, no woman alive was good enough for her son. Second, Leah had no dowry. As far as Sarah was concerned, the impending marriage spelled nothing but doom. But her son was smitten, and as soon as the two were married, Sarah begrudgingly caught glimpses of Leah's true soul. What she saw was beauty both inside and out, although she refused to admit it.

So they had lived as a family for more than four years. Only one cloud shadowed their happiness. Leah and Daniel had no children. It was no small event when Leah learned she was pregnant with their first child. Happiness beamed around every corner. Leah was to be a mother, Daniel a father, and Sarah a grandmother. Then came the events of that unhappy day, and since then, happiness was the most elusive gift of all.

Daniel and Leah had buried their son, Benjamin, beneath the angel catching tree, beside his grandmother Elisabeth.

Rebuilding Leah's happiness became Daniel's mission in life. He knew how much she wanted children, and he felt responsible that they had such difficulties. There had to have been something he could have done to save their child. Was it a lack of faith, or was there something wrong with him that had been passed to the baby?

Daniel brought himself back to the present with a shake, accepting that his heart was laden with questions for which he would never know the answer. He slowly got up from his resting place beneath the tree to tackle the task at hand. He needed to prepare the stable for guests. It wasn't uncommon for guests to stay in the stable when some occasion or other filled Bethlehem to the brim. With the inn already full, Daniel was certain someone would need the stable. He would clean it and make sure there was room for blankets to be spread upon the hay. The few animals Daniel kept eyed him suspiciously. Sharing their stable meant they would be on a much shorter tether to make room for the human guests, and strange animals that smelled of far-off places would be brought in to share their home.

Daniel brushed aside a swatch of hay, and suddenly his world crashed to a halt. Emotions he had never known he had overwhelmed him. Tears ran down his face as he fell to his knees, sobbing, and brushed away the rest of the hay from the small wooden object. It was the unfinished cradle. He felt the wood that he had carefully carved, etching designs of the desert into the side of the cradle. The workmanship wasn't as fine as the cradles that could be purchased from the marketplace, yet the cradle revealed a beauty only a father's hands could give. He wept openly as he remembered that unforgiving day when he laid his son in the ground instead of in the cradle he had so lovingly formed. In his grief he had hurriedly buried the cradle in the hay.

He knelt in front of the cradle and spread open his fingers, seeing there the few scars that were the result of his clumsiness with woodworking. He buried his face in his hands, frightened by the intensity of the feelings that coursed through him, leaving his body shaking and heaving with raw emotion.

"Daniel?"

Daniel turned to see Leah outlined in shadow against the stable door, the sun shining through her hair like smoking embers.

"Leah!" Daniel gasped. "Please, leave me be."

"What's happened? Are you hurt?"

"Leah," he pleaded, "I'm not hurt. I just need some time alone. I don't want you to see me like this."

Leah knelt behind him, placing her hands on his shoulders.

"I won't leave you. I can't leave you like this . . " Leah stopped abruptly as her eyes grew accustomed to the shadows and she saw the cradle. She sighed and slid onto the ground, leaning against Daniel.

"Leah, I'm so sorry," he said.

"There's nothing to be sorry about, Daniel.

It's the most beautiful cradle we could have used for our son."

"Not about the cradle, Leah. I'm sorry about me . . us. I've ruined your life, stolen your beauty. You don't belong here in a stable behind an old inn, married to a man I can't imagine you've ever really loved, a man who can't even give you what you want most of all . . , children, even one child."

"Daniel, how could you believe it's your fault? It is I who failed us.

"Don't you see, Leah? My mother only could have one child.. the problem must be in my family. If you had married someone else, you could have had as many children as you wanted. Instead, you'll grow old with just an innkeeper for company. The baby, our baby, was my gift to you. He was the one thing I could give you that we could share, that would be part of us. We would have reared that child to be caring and gentle, and then the child could be our gift to the world, the best parts of you and me."

Leah felt a surge of love for Daniel, hearing him revealing things she had never imagined. She had been so wrapped up in her grief that she couldn't see past her own needs. Here was her husband, the one man she loved in the world, and only now was she finding out the devastation the loss of their child had wreaked upon him. She drew him to her and held him close.

His words continued. "This cradle was meant to safeguard our child. It was in this cradle he would have heard our voices singing him to sleep. All I ever wanted was to love our little Benjamin, to keep him safe and sheltered. Now he sleeps only in our hearts, and this cradle, his cradle, is cold and useless."

Leah reached over and once again covered the unfinished cradle with hay.

"Shhhh," she said to Daniel as she cradled him in her arms. "We'll make it through this. We'll make it through together."

Chapter Four

Ardis lay on the floor of the kitchen, peering out into the dining area. Daniel tripped over her legs in the process.

"What are you doing?" he asked.

"Peeking," said Ardis matter-of-factly.

"At whom?"

"At that old woman."

"My mother? Don't let her hear you talking like that," replied Daniel. "She thinks you're enough trouble as it is."

"No, not your mother. That old lady in the dining room, the pretty one."

Daniel had just been in the dining room and had seen no one there like that. "Move over," he said to Ardis as he knelt down beside her and carefully peeked out into the dining room himself.

The old woman saw only the eyes of a young girl close to the floor of the doorway. A foot or so above her came a much larger set of eyes preceded by a big, balding head. She smiled and winked at the both of them. The balding head immediately pulled back into the kitchen, but the little set of eyes returned the wink and giggled.

"You didn't tell me she was peeking back!" said a mortified Daniel.

"You didn't ask," Ardis replied.

"Daniel?"

Daniel looked up to see his mother glaring at them disapprovingly.

"What are you doing down there?" she demanded.

Daniel had no better reply than the truth.

"Peeking," he said.

Sarah was flustered for a moment, not knowing what to say. Daniel leaned back against the wall and shrugged apologetically to Sarah.

"Well, stop it," she said as she swept past them.

"I think she's somebody's grandma," said Ardis as Leah walked into the room.

"Is there a reason you're on the floor at this very busy moment?" asked Leah, apparently not particularly surprised to see them there.

Daniel pulled Ardis away from the door and put his arm around her conspiratorially.

"We have our reasons, and we prefer to keep our reasons to ourselves," he said as Ardis giggled some more. "We seem to have a new customer out there. Do you mind tending to her?"

Leah looked out the door and saw the old woman, who was looking right back at her.

"Why?" asked Leah.

"I have my reasons," replied Daniel sheepishly.

Leah sized up the woman as she walked toward her table. The elderly woman projected a spirit of inner strength. She held herself with great poise, which took Leah aback for a moment. She was so reminiscent of Leah's own mother.

"Is that your little girl?" asked the woman, though Leah sensed the woman already knew the answer to the question.

"No. The only child I can lay claim to is the big, bearded one in there," replied Leah laughingly, then she felt a pang of regret for a moment as she thought of her lost baby boy.

Pain crossed her face and was very evident to the old woman. Leah shook it off as well as she could.

"Something wrong?" asked the old woman.

"Nothing that time won't heal," replied Leah, struggling to put on a pleasant face for her customer.

"There are some things time doesn't heal," said the old woman. "Time only allows us time to try to understand, try to learn what our experiences are meant to teach us," she continued carefully, searching Leah's face for a response, "time to find the miracles in ourselves."

Leah's eyes filled with tears as she dealt with the grief, anger, and hope the old woman's words stirred inside her. She sat beside the woman, bowing her head so the other customers couldn't see her tears. The old woman took one of Leah's hands in her own, saying nothing. Leah alternated between resentment and gratitude as the old woman caressed her fingers.

"I . . . I'm sorry," apologized Leah, and against her will she found herself revealing her experience to the old woman. "It's just that I lost a baby recently, and it's difficult to see the miracles right now, or even hope for them."

"I understand," said the old woman. "Life itself is one of the biggest miracles of all, and the journey to life is fraught with peril. Many can't complete the journey, no matter how much they desire it or others may want them to. You should know how blessed you are merely to have received the gift of life or to have given it, no matter how briefly. That alone is a miracle."

Leah looked into the old woman's eyes, captivated by the wisdom that emanated from them. Then she wrested back control of her senses. She didn't even know who this woman was or why she felt she could talk so personally with her. The old woman sensed this change in Leah and changed the subject.

"I'm here myself for a babe to be born. I've come to bring a gift to the child."

"A relative?" asked Leah.

"Most definitely," said the old woman. " It will be a most glorious birth. I promise you, it will be a miracle you won't forget."

"Ah," replied Leah, distancing herself further from the woman. It was too difficult for her to believe in miracles now. Her attention was drawn from the old woman when she heard Daniel talking to someone at the door.

"Excuse me," she said to the woman as she left the table and walked to the door.

"I'm sorry, the inn is full. We have no room for you," Daniel was saying as Leah walked up behind him. A woman sat upon a donkey, guided by a very concerned man whom Leah took to be the woman's husband. The woman was great with child, and Leah's heart went out to her.

"Do you have any space at all?" asked the man. "My wife needs to rest. We've had a long journey and can't find anyplace to stay."

Daniel felt compassion for them both. He could see the young woman was in great physical discomfort and the man was beside himself with worry.

"Give me a moment," said Daniel. "Perhaps we could work something out."

Daniel shut the door for a moment.

"How about our room?" he asked. Leah couldn't bear the thought of another birth there so soon. If they gave them their room, she feared she would have to leave the inn to defend her own fragile well-being. She couldn't do that when the inn was so full. Besides, her husband would be torn apart by the experience, though he would put on a stoic face and help as much as he could. Still, perhaps, it was the right thing to do.

"They can have the stable," interjected Sarah, who had been listening from the kitchen.

"The stable?" replied Daniel. "For someone about to give birth?"

"It's warm and dry, they'll have a roof over

their heads, a place for fire, and water. It certainly is much better than the open desert," said Sarah.

Perhaps she's right, thought Daniel. They could still help the young couple and protect themselves as well. He was relieved that his mother had made the decision. Leah averted her eyes. He sensed that she, too, was relieved. He opened the door again.

"It's not much, but we do have our stable to offer you. We've prepared it as best we can for travelers."

"We'd be grateful for it," replied the man.

Daniel led the couple to the stable as Leah watched them through the window. She felt regret as she saw how difficult it was for the woman to dismount the donkey. Then the woman looked directly up at her, and Leah's heart raced. She felt she knew this woman, that they shared a common bond. The woman smiled warmly at Leah as her husband took her arm and helped her through the stable door.

Leah stayed at the window while emotions

warred inside her. Then she remembered the old woman and turned back to her. The old woman was nowhere to be seen.

Chapter Five

Ardis stood open-mouthed on the bluff outside her family's tent, holding her rag doll tightly to her as she watched the light beam from behind the surrounding hills. Her heart filled with a mixture of joy and confusion as the voices of a choir filled the earth with their resonance. She was still there long after the light faded and watched her father scramble up the hillside towards her. When he drew near she could see the tears streaming down his face.

"Did you see them?' he puffed as he tried to regain his breath.

"See whom?" asked Ardis.

"Did you at least hear them?" her father asked.

"Hear whom?" demanded Ardis.

Ardis's father swung her up and around and into his arms.

"Come," he said. "We have little time."

"Daddy! Where are we going?" cried Ardis, a little frightened by her father's erratic behavior. Just then she saw her shadow burst brilliantly in front of her, and she turned her head as the light of the most brilliant and beautiful star she had ever seen climbed the night sky and stood sentry at the apex of the heavens. The light from the star shone directly down and seemed to envelop Bethlehem in its arms. Ardis's father drew her closer to him, and she could feel the warmth of his tears against her cheek.

"There," he said, pointing. "We are going there."

. . . .

Leah awakened as she felt the bed lean to one side. Without even opening her eyes, she knew Daniel was sitting on the side of the bed with his head down.

"What's wrong?" she asked.

"Nothing. Just restless, I guess," replied Daniel.

Leah stared blankly into the dim room, finding solace in the familiarity of the dim shapes of their furniture and belongings. She was just beginning to accept the bedroom as a refuge against the world once again, a place where she could share intimacies and hopes without the outside world looking on or judging. The memories connected with the birth of Benjamin were becoming distant enough that time was starting to make the agony bearable. How grateful she was that Sarah had not allowed them close contact with the family in the stable. They would be fine, she thought. Most likely the child would be born elsewhere, and the stable would be just a spot in which to rest from their journey.

The floorboards creaked, and Leah knew that Daniel had risen and was putting on his clothes. The soft rustling of the fabric was such a soothing sound, but Leah's stomach tightened with unease.

"Daniel, don't," she said.

"Don't what?" asked Daniel. "I'm just going to check the hearth and make sure everything is all right downstairs."

"I know you better than that, Daniel. You're going to the stable, aren't you?'

Daniel sighed. He should have known he couldn't hide much from Leah. After all they'd been through, they'd finally grown accustomed to each others' hearts.

"Yes, but just to see if there's anything to be done. Hopefully they're asleep, and I'll be back in a few minutes," said Daniel.

He paused at the doorway, waiting to see if Leah would say anything else. Then he returned to sit by her side, stroking her hair, saying nothing. It was several minutes before Leah could speak.

"I know I should have let them have our bedroom, but I couldn't face it. This room should be filled with the laughter and sounds of our own son, not the sounds of a strange child just entering life."

"Shhhh," said Daniel. "Everything is all right, the stable is clean and warm, and they'll be leaving soon."

"What would happen if this child died, too?" said Leah. "Could you come into this room again? I don't think I could. I don't think I could even bear to come inside the inn again."

Daniel leaned down and kissed her on the

forehead. "Go back to sleep. I'll be back in a while."

Leah reached out and grabbed his hand, not wanting him to leave. Daniel gently removed her hand from his and smiled once again to reassure her. He walked quickly out of the room. Leah closed her eyes and drew the bedclothes tight around her but refused to sleep until Daniel came back. But as the minutes waxed on, the familiar fog came once again across her mind and she drifted toward sleep.

Suddenly there was light. Brilliant light. Leah could see light through the lids of her eyes. Thinking she must have fallen asleep and the morning sun was bearing down on her, she opened her eyes, but the rest of the room was shrouded in darkness. A single beam of light shot through the window and rested on the bed. She shielded her eyes from it and slowly walked to the window, quite sure she was dreaming, for this light was more luminous than that of any candle or fire.

In the sky there shone a star, larger and brighter than any she had seen before, and though it surely was impossible, the star blazed directly above the stable behind the inn, bathing it with an illumination so vivid it seemed to bear not only light but love. The stable was the epicenter, and the light reached down from the heavens above and cradled the stable in bliss.

Now Leah was sure she was dreaming, and that realization loosened her inhibitions. Instinctively she closed her eyes and reached out. A shard of light broke off and bathed her in love, warming her heart, and clarifying her soul. She felt that the light could lift her into the heavens, and from that starry perch she could look down on the world beneath her and understand life and love, and why death, hate, and sorrow were allowed to exist. She opened her eyes again and gazed directly into the light. A small beam drifted free from the star and floated towards her, growing larger as it got closer. Leah cried out and leapt back when she realized the beam of light was a person. She stumbled and fell hard against the floor, rapping her head sharply on the bedpost. Though she felt the solid floor and experienced the momentary pain in her head, she realized this wasn't a dream after all. "But it has to be a dream," she said aloud to herself, trying to will away the luminous image that stood before her.

"This is not a dream, Leah. It is a miracle, but it's no dream."

Leah shook, but as she looked into the radiance of the image before her, she realized her shaking was not from fear but from witnessing the radiant power of pure love. The person before her was a woman who seemed oddly familiar to Leah. Then it dawned on her that although whoever stood before her seemed ageless, even angelic, it was the old woman she had spoken to earlier that day in the inn.

"Yes," said the woman, as if she knew Leah's every thought, "you're right. I am an angel, a messenger sent to bring you tidings of great joy. I promised you a miracle you would never forget."

At that moment, they could hear the cry of

a newborn babe as it gasped life into its lungs.

"I also promised you a glorious birth," said the angel, and both she and Leah turned toward the sounds emanating from the stable as life itself was trumpeted by the cry of the babe.

"Behold," said the angel, "your King and your Savior."

Leah examined the face of the angel as she realized what she had done.

"Is he . . . ," Leah turned her eyes from the angel before she completed her question, afraid of the answer and fearing the consequences, "is he the Messiah?"

The angel answered simply, "He is."

"Then," cried out Leah, "I have turned the Son of God away from my door! I refused him shelter!"

Her heart rent in agony as the full realization of what she had done settled in. She writhed in confusion and pain, praying now that this was a dream, that she had not done such an unforgivable thing. Then the thought of her own mother entered her mind, the memories of all the times her mother had held her and told her of the Messiah that was to come. What would her mother have done, thought Leah, if she had known her daughter would be the one to turn away the Messiah at the very moment of his birth?

"All the answers are in your heart, Leah. They are miracles, and they belong to everyone. Some are small and some are large, but all are waiting to be given life. They are born of faith and love and can heal the depths of every wound. Faith and love, Leah."

Leah jerked her head up sharply and looked at the angel. The angel was smiling, and as she smiled, Leah's heart felt a healing warmth start from the inside out.

"Yes," comforted the angel, "your mother is a very wise woman, a woman of faith, and a woman of love, just as you are."

The angel touched the side of Leah's face. "God understands. God understands more than you could ever possibly imagine, but he needs you to understand, too. Where there is understanding, there is faith, and where there is faith, there is love. You cannot understand without experiencing, and just as you have experienced the loss of a child, within your lifetime you will also understand the gift and the sacrifice God has made to the world. Faith and love, Leah. Faith and love."

Leah began to sob as she felt the unconditional love that flowed from the angel to her, healing long-held wounds and filling voids in her soul that she hadn't even known were there. The angel raised Leah to her feet.

"I told you I had come to bring a gift for the newborn babe," said the angel. "My gift to him is your renewed faith and love, Leah. These gifts outshine any earthly gift that could be given to one such as he."

The angel motioned toward the stable "Go, Leah, go and behold your King."

The woman's angelic iridescence swirled about Leah, confirming to the very depths of her heart and soul that what the angel told her was true. Then the angel's light drifted back again towards the heavens, melding into the effulgent radiance cradling the stable.

Chapter Six

Daniel closed the door of the stable behind him and leaned against the wall. His knees buckled from the glory he had experienced within the humble walls behind him. He drew himself up, walked over to the olive tree, and leaned his back against it, slowly sliding to the ground as he had done hundreds of times before. He caught his breath when the light from the brilliant star above danced through the branches of the tree framing the graves of his son and his mother-in-law. Bursting into his heart came a sure knowledge that these small plots of earth were not the final resting place of those whose mortal bodies laid within. Although he couldn't see them, he could feel the presence of his son, Benjamin, wrapped in the arms of his grandmother, as they whirled and danced about the yard in joyous celebration. Tears of joy streamed down Daniel's face as he exulted in the moment of communion between heaven and earth.

Leah threw open the door of the inn and ran out into the yard. She shielded her eyes until they became accustomed to the brilliance around her. She felt the luminescence that surrounded her was more than light, it was a presence that filled her heart with peace. It was an illuminated spirit, realized Leah, the pure spirit of God's glory emanating truth, a spirit that coursed through her body and filled her with joy. She saw Daniel sitting at the base of the olive tree. She embraced him, knowing that he was feeling what she was. Leah watched with him as the light danced about the yard, and the Spirit bore witness to her that her Benjamin and her mother were not dead, but had merely passed on to another glory. Daniel held her hand to his cheek and then, without a word, released it so she could go to the stable and behold the child within.

The familiar smell of warm hay and animals filled the air that rushed past her face as she opened the door, in stark contrast to the glory of the light from the star illuminating the courtyard. The first thing that caught Leah's eye was the cradle the babe lay in. It was the one Daniel had made for Benjamin. For a moment, Leah's heart felt the familiar pang of sorrow, but the sorrow turned to wonder as her eyes beheld the child in the cradle, wrapped in swaddling clothes. Only a very few were within the stable, the mother and father of the child, and several shepherds kneeling. Leah herself knelt quickly when she saw the others, but the mother of the babe motioned to her husband, and he took Leah by her elbow, raising her and bringing her closer to the cradle.

"You are welcome here. This is my wife, Mary, and I am Joseph," he said.

Leah, now coming face to face with the woman whom they had turned away from their door, cast her eyes to the ground, startled by abrupt emotions that now filled her with shame.

"I am. . , I . . ," mumbled Leah, realizing that now she wanted to leave, to run from the peace that filled the room, needing to escape the love that filled the eyes of the woman before her, the woman she had shunned. Leah collapsed in shame and sorrow, sobbing and pleading, "Forgive me, Mary, Joseph. He should have been born in my bed."

"Shh," said Mary. "You have nothing to be forgiven for. If our Father in Heaven had wanted His child to be born in your bed, he would have been. But if this babe had been born in your bed, then generation upon generation of holy prophecy would have gone unfulfilled. God is watching over this child, and His works will be accomplished as He sees fit."

Leah struggled to believe in her words, wanting them to be true. She needed to believe that her actions were actually a part of God's plan and not just a selfish act. Mary deftly put her hand under Leah's chin and gently raised her head until their eyes met.

"You have nothing to be sorry for, Leah"

Leah lifted her head, surprised that Mary knew her name.

"Daniel told us about you as he helped us prepare the cradle," Mary explained. "He loves you very much, and is quite proud to be your husband." She smiled.

Leah, softened by Mary's easy conversation, allowed herself to look into Mary's eyes. She could see how tired she was, how much of a toll the birth had taken on her. Leah quickly prepared a few blankets for Mary to lie back upon and rest. Mary took Leah's hand for support as she lay back. Leah could feel Mary's strength, but at this moment, she could also feel how vulnerable she was. Mary was grateful for the help of a kindred soul. Mary reached into the bundle of cloth that wrapped her babe and drew out a small chubby hand, perfectly pink and delicate beyond belief. Putting the tiny hand into Leah's, Mary said, "And this is my son, Jesus."

Leah could hardly breathe as she felt the newborn skin of the tiny hand. Instinctively, she rolled each little finger between her own fingers.

"They're all there," Mary chuckled as she recognized that Leah was doing what she herself had done just a short time before. Leah was overcome by a desire to hold the child, to nestle the baby close to her bosom, to smell the tiny curls of hair and cradle the babe in her arms. She was afraid, though, afraid of what emotions might overtake her as she held a baby for the first time since she had held her own little Benjamin. Nevertheless, pushing past her fears, she asked with tears in her eyes, "Mary, may I hold your baby?"

Mary said nothing but gently scooped the child out of the cradle and tenderly placed him in Leah's arms. Leah fought back tears as she couldn't help but compare the feel of this baby that was so full of life with the last time she had held her own little Benjamin. She tenderly raised the babe and put her cheek against his, holding him as tightly as she dared, breathing in deeply the sweet scent that only newborns have. As she felt his pliant little body mold to hers, she could feel the healing power of God. Leah felt life's burdens leaving her as she embraced Mary's son. Without being aware of it, the baby Jesus had just performed his first miracle. He gave back to Leah something she could not have lived without, hope for the future.

With that hope now in her heart, Leah longed for another child. For a brief moment, she envied Mary. She held the baby Jesus as close as she dared and wished in her heart that for just a brief moment, this baby could actually be hers. Her thought was interrupted by the sound of Mary's voice.

"God is not finished with you," Mary said. "You will hold your child again, and many others will be given to you. You are to be blessed, Leah, blessed beyond anything you can understand. Faith and love, Leah. Faith and love."

It was no longer a surprise to Leah to hear the words of her mother from what seemed like so long ago. She placed Jesus back in the cradle, making sure every tiny part of him was well covered and protected. Then she took Mary's hand. "Thank you for sharing your Son not only with me but with the world."

As Leah wiped the tears from her eyes, the stable door opened. In walked Daniel and Sarah bearing plates of food for Joseph and Mary. Behind them came in reverently many who had gathered in the inn's courtyard to see the Christ child, brought there by the brilliant star that stood as a sentinel in the sky above. Among them, still perched high upon her father's shoulders, was Ardis, clutching her rag doll. Leah motioned for her to come closer, and Ardis scrambled down off her father's shoulders and eagerly approached the cradle.

"Mary and Joseph, I'd like you to meet someone who is very special to our family," Leah said. "This is Ardis."

"Hello, Ardis," said Mary.

Ardis fidgeted for a moment, and then blurted out "Is it a girl or is it a boy?"

"He's a little boy," replied Mary. "His name is Jesus."

"Lots of people have presents for him," said Ardis, her eyes looking down at her rag doll as she rocked back and forth on her feet. It was one of the few times in her life that she was at a loss for words, but Leah could tell what was on her mind.

"Did you want to give him a present, too?" asked Leah.

Ardis just squirmed some more and nodded yes.

"Is it your rag doll you want to give him?" Leah asked again.

Leah told Mary, "Her mother made it for her when she was a baby, and she's had it ever since. It goes everywhere with her."

"That would explain why it looks, uh, so well loved," smiled Mary with a twinkle in her eye. "Are you sure you want him to have it?"

"I'm sure," replied Ardis. "I needed it when I was a baby, but now I'm a big girl."

Ardis knelt beside the cradle and gently nestled the rag doll close by Jesus' side.

"She's very well behaved, and she'll listen to anything you want to tell her," Ardis whispered to baby Jesus. "She always keeps a secret. Best of all, she'll cuddle whenever you need to."

Ardis got up, and with tears in her eyes leaned over and kissed Jesus on his cheek. Mary wrapped her in her arms and hugged her tight.

"Thank you," Mary said to Ardis. "Thank you for giving him a friend."

Ardis continued to fight back her tears.

"It's only a rag doll," she said.

"I didn't mean the doll," replied Mary. "I meant you. He's going to need a lot of friends just like you, willing to give up their most precious things to help him."

Ardis burst into tears and held onto Mary. Leah gently took her and hugged her, and then walked her back to her father. Her father picked her up and let her cry into his ample chest. Leah and Daniel, knowing Mary, Joseph and Jesus needed rest, coaxed every one into the inn for refreshments. When the stable was nearly empty, Leah took Mary's hand.

"If the need should ever arise," she said, "count me as your sister."

Mary squeezed Leah's hand. "And you the same."

Chapter Seven

Leah leaned her head back and let the Spirit wash over her. After all these months, there was still a peace in this place that could only be described as holiness. Leah opened her eyes and watched as small shards of sunlight broke away from the cracks in the roof and walls, randomly illuminating her surroundings. For a moment she could see the floor, and then it was gone, replaced by a glimpse of the rustic door latch. Leah gasped as the light first rested and then stayed on the very thing she had come to the stable to find: the cradle fashioned by the hands of her dear Daniel and lain upon by Jesus, the son of Mary.

She laughed at herself for a moment for gasping at such a find. Should she expect anything else? Small miracles like this were everyday fare for her now. She had come not only to expect them but also to recognize them. At the end of the day, she would kneel with her husband, and together they would thank God for the miracles they had experienced.

Leah knelt in silence before the cradle and slowly wiped off the dust. It was the first time she had touched anything inside the stable since their guests of that heavenly night had left. As her hands caressed the wood, Leah thought of the days beyond the Savior's birth. Try as she might, neither she nor Daniel could convince Joseph and Mary to come and stay inside the inn. Mary insisted that for her there could be no place sweeter than the place where her child was born. So Leah and Daniel worked extra hours to keep the inn running and also to make sure the stable stayed clean and hospitable.

Leah and Mary had shared much with each other, and Leah felt that in Mary she truly did have a sister. Mary felt the same. In the quiet hours when Mary was nursing her baby, she and Leah talked in hushed tones about the great miracles in store for the small babe. In those first few days of his life, neither Mary nor Leah could think of anything but good happening to this tiny boy. Meanwhile, Joseph and Daniel readied their animals and packs for the traveling that was now before the young couple and the baby.

Leah picked up the cradle, wondering how she would ever get it into the house, because it took all her strength just to lift it on top of the hay. Just then she heard a familiar voice singing a song at the top of her lungs as she made her way towards the inn. Mary hurried out the stable door and saw Ardis about twenty yards away from the inn. She motioned until she caught Ardis' eye and then darted back into the stable when she saw Daniel coming out of the inn.

"Leah?" called Ardis into the darkness of the closed stable.

"Did Daniel see you?" replied Leah, just a few feet from Ardis but well hidden in the darkness.

"No."

Ardis gasped when a pair of hands grasped her shoulders, drew her into the stable, and then quickly shut the door behind her. Ardis was now in complete darkness for all intents and purposes, her eyes not having become accustomed yet to the deep shadows of the stable.

"Leah, you're scaring me. Are you all right?" asked Ardis, only half in jest.

"Yes, my dear girl," replied Leah. "I need your help."

"For what?"

Ardis' eyes were becoming accustomed to the dark by now. Leah led her to the cradle and put her hand on it.

"We need to get this up the stairs and into Daniel's and my bedroom."

"Why?"

"Because we do, that's why."

"ARDIS!" called Daniel from the inn door.

"Don't answer him," cautioned Leah.

"But if I don't, he'll come looking for me."

"Okay, you're right. Go and tell him his mother needs your help."

Ardis crept to the door, caught up in the excitement of whatever was going on. She peeked out and then ran quickly back to the road, to approach the front of the inn as if she had just arrived. Smart girl, thought Leah, as she watched Ardis from a crack in the stable wall. Daniel opened the door for her and then followed her inside.

Leah stood watch at the door for what

seemed like hours but in actuality were only minutes. She sighed with relief when Ardis finally came out the door and stared in disbelief when Sarah followed a few steps behind her. Both made their way to the stable.

"Leah?" Ardis softly called into the darkness of the stable as she opened the door quickly and ushered Sarah in behind her.

"Leah?" queried Sarah as her eyes started to accustom themselves to the lack of light.

Leah stood up from behind the cradle.

"Good morning, Mother Sarah," she said in resignation.

Ardis chimed in, "I did exactly what you told me. I told Daniel his mother needed my help."

"I knew I didn't ask for her help," added Sarah, "so I asked where I needed her help, and she brought me here."

"So here we all are," offered Leah, not knowing what else to say.

"Can't she help us move the cradle?" asked Ardis.

"Cradle?" inquired Sarah.

"I don't have a choice now," said Leah. "Mother Sarah, could you please help us move this cradle up to Daniel's and my bedroom?"

"Why would you want you want . . ," began Sarah, until the reason dawned on her.

"Do you mean . . , are you saying . .," sputtered Sarah.

"I guess I am," said Leah simply, feeling she'd been caught in her own web.

Leah was not prepared for Sarah's reaction. For that matter, Sarah was not prepared for Sarah's reaction, and Ardis, not having any idea of what either one of them was talking about, was absolutely floored when Sarah burst into tears and embraced Leah as if she were embracing her very own daughter. Sarah laughed and cried at the same time. Leah laughed and cried also. Ardis watched them in amazement.

Sarah kissed Leah on the cheek. "This makes me so happy for you, and Daniel, too, of course. It's about time . . ."

Sarah was cut off in mid-sentence when
the door burst open. There stood Daniel. In
the dim light he could make out the figures of
Ardis, Sarah, and Leah. He thought that the
dark must be playing tricks on him, because
he could swear his mother was embracing
Leah and Leah was returning the embrace.

"Leah? Mother?"

Sarah immediately took Leah's arm and
pushed her and Daniel out the door.

"Daniel, I think you should take your wife
for a walk."

Leah started to say, "What about . . ?"

"Don't worry," said Sarah, "Everything
will be taken care of when you get back home.
Ardis and I will do just fine."

About twenty minutes later, Daniel and Leah
returned to the inn. Leah took Daniel's hand
and led him upstairs to their room. Not
knowing what to think, he walked into the room
and over to the window. He couldn't believe

what he saw. There, sitting on the ground with their backs against the olive tree, were Sarah and Ardis, and Sarah's arms were wrapped around Ardis, holding her as they talked.

"I'll be," said Daniel. "I never thought I'd see this."

Leah, looking over his shoulder at the scene below, whispered in his ear, "Faith and love, Daniel. That's all it takes for a miracle or two. Faith and love."

She kissed his hand and led him to the corner of the room where

Sarah and Ardis had been hard at work. There was the cradle dressed with blankets, pillows, and flowers. Daniel was confused for just a moment, and then he grabbed Leah by the waist.

"Are you?" he screamed in delight.

Leah nodded yes, and Daniel shouted as he whirled her about the room, over and over again.

Hearing Daniel's excitement, Sarah and Ardis looked up towards the bedroom window and saw the twirling figures.

"I wish someone would tell me what's going on," Ardis griped in exasperation.

Knowing Leah would want to tell her herself, Sarah just hugged the girl and said, "Life, Ardis. Life is what's going on."

Epilogue

It was late in the fall when I sat down at my piano to write a new song for the approaching Christmas season. As my hands struck the keys, I found myself singing the words, Mary, may I hold Him? With my eyes closed and the music flowing, I was playing the song as if I had known it my entire life. I envisioned the stable and all of it's surroundings. Then with a rush of emotion I saw Leah reach out her hands to hold the Christ child. At that moment I was filled with pure emotion as the tears ran down my face and into my heart. I wanted to hold him, too. The rest of the story flooded my mind.

I had always wondered why the innkeeper and his wife had not offered their bed to Mary on that night so long ago. For the next several days all I could think about was the story and its main characters, and I continued to write the music. Lyrics and music have always taken me great time to put together, but not in this case. The melodies continued to flow and the words followed right behind. It was an amazing time for me, with many sleepless nights. After writing *Leah's Theme*, *Heaven's Lullaby*, *May I Hold Him*, and revising *My Child, My Love*, I had grown even closer to the story and its characters. With each song I began to realize that I was being handed something unique and much bigger than I had imagined. It truly had a spirit of its own.

One night stands out brighter than the rest for me. I often went to play the piano at a nearby chapel. While enjoying a moment of peace in the day I sat quietly in the back of the chapel with my eyes closed. A vivid picture of a little girl who was following some shepherds appeared ever so clearly in my mind. She had a rag doll in her hands and curiosity in her heart. Upon her arrival to the stable she was immediately drawn to the baby Jesus, and pushed her way through the crowd. The little girl gently kissed his head as she placed the doll in his cradle and tearfully walked off. Within the next half hour I had written *Take My Rag Doll* in perfect form. Several days later I was having the doll made.

I knew that the music and the doll were important, and now it was time for the story to become a book. It all had such a recognizable healing power buried within it. It was a story that needed to be shared.

With no intention of writing the book alone, I began to look for a writer to pen my story. Through the course of events and many telephone calls I found Nyle. Through his life of miracles and experiences the story would find its true form on paper.

That story and it's elements of magic were now engraved in my mind, through many more sleepless nights. It began to open my heart as it taught me about miracles and the desperate need for hope in this world. I was beginning to understand the grace and power that miracles truly hold.

Within the past year I had watched and

heard of several friends whose young children had died. I sang at some of the funerals and was extremely moved by the parents' courage and emotion. One week before Christmas a college roommate called me with the news of her young son's death. She wanted me to sing at his funeral. In the moments I watched her and her husband say such an early good-bye something powerful sank into my heart. It was the thought that miracles are born of love and handed to us by our faith. Their son Robbie had come as a miracle, and his early departure home to God would lend itself to teaching faith for further miracles. Not just for their family, but for all those who would be touched by their example and lives. It changed our Christmas season forever.

The spirit of this story, born through music and the inspired words that Nyle put on paper, is one of healing, hope, and all of love's miracles. Miracles are another facet of love's power. They sometimes are the arms that hold us, or the soft words that grace our hearts. There are times we cant even see them until they fulfill their purpose. Nevertheless, in whatever form they come, they are all wondrous.

We're all part of a miracle called life. In this life we are given the chance to love and to be loved. Love is a gift. God gave the world faith and love beyond compare when he allowed us to behold his Son in a rocky stable lit by heaven's light so long ago. A night embraced by choirs of angels and lullabies for a King. Under that same starlit sky a young girl became a mother. Mary, chosen above all others to act as heavens arms on earth, would give her son to the world. Through His life, love would bear it's greatest purpose. It was a miracle of faith and love . . . the miracle we call Christmas.

S.K.

Song Lyrics

My Child, My Love

Take My Rag Doll

May I Hold Him

My Child, My Love

S.Krupa

(Copyright 1993)

I cradled you in my arms
When you were sent to me
For only a moment
And then you were free

Oh how I miss you
And long to see your face
But I had to let you go
Home to God's embrace

My child, my love
My life, my son
Baby of mine
Angel divine
Back to your Father's arms

I kissed each little finger
And watched you close your eyes
Before the heavens took you
Away for just awhile
My heart now will hold you
Until you're by my side
I pray the angels
Will sing for you
This mothers lullaby

My child, my love
My life, my son
Baby of mine
Angel divine
Back to your Father's arms

Baby of mine
Angel divine
Back to your Father's arms.

(New lullaby version lyrics S.Krupa
& V. Pahnke Copyright 1996)

Take My Rag Doll

S.Krupa

I don't know if you can hear me Lord
I'm a child just like You
I saw some shepherds
Leaving their fields
So I followed them to You

I don't have silver or gold that I can give You
But You can have my heart

Take my rag doll
Hold it close to You
My mamma made her
When I was small like You
Though I will miss her
I'll always think of You
Take my rag doll

Keep her safe with You

When I grow old
Will I see you again
And will You hold me
Like my doll
I will kiss You
And say good-bye
Even though
I know it's just for now

How I will miss you my King
My heart can feel it
Cause You have changed my life

Please take my rag doll
And hold it close to You
My mamma made her
When I was small like You
I will miss her
But I'll remember You
Holding my rag doll
Close to You
Please keep my rag doll
Close to You.

(Copyright 1996)

May I Hold Him

S.Krupa

(Leah)
Mary, may I hold Him
Miracle divine?
One moment, just to love Him
Safely in my arms
I turned you away
Closed my door
And still you let me in
Please forgive me, forgive me

(Mary)
Leah, this is Jesus
Hold Him like He's yours
He comes as
Heaven's miracle
He comes to save us all

Open your heart
Breathe the spirit in
And my sister you will know
That He loves you
My son loves you

(Both)
We'll be friends
For more than just one night
That I promise you
As this time ends
Love keeps us friends

(Leah)
Mary, I will love Him

(Mary)
And He will love you too

(Leah)
Oh, how I will adore Him
Christ My Lord

(Copyright 1996)

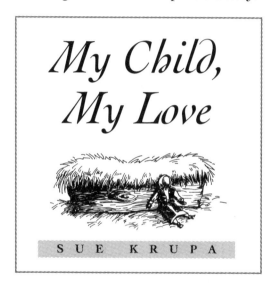